¡Hola, ¡Lola!

Bad Luck Lola

BY KEKA NOVALES

ILLUSTRATED BY GLORIA FÉLIX

PICTURE WINDOW BOOKS
a capstone imprint

Published by Picture Window Books, an imprint of Capstone.
1710 Roe Crest Drive, North Mankato, Minnesota 56003
capstonepub.com

Library of Congress Cataloging-in-Publication Data
Names: Novales, Keka, author. | Félix, Gloria, illustrator.
Title: Bad luck Lola / by Keka Novales; illustrated by Gloria Félix.
Description: North Mankato, Minnesota : Picture Window Books,
an imprint of Capstone, 2022. | Series: ¡Hola, Lola! | Audience: Ages
5–7. | Audience: Grades K–1. | Text primarily in English; some words
in Spanish. | Summary: When Lola cracks a mirror, she is not worried
at first, but when one unlucky thing after another happens, Lola slowly
becomes convinced she is cursed.
Identifiers: LCCN 2021056946 (print) | LCCN 2021056947 (ebook) |
ISBN 9781666337273 (hardcover) | ISBN 9781666343908 (paperback) |
ISBN 9781666343946 (pdf)
Subjects: LCSH: Superstition—Juvenile fiction. | Fortune—Juvenile
fiction. | Guatemalan Americans—Juvenile fiction. | CYAC:
Superstition—Fiction. | Luck—Fiction. | Guatemalan Americans—
Fiction. | LCGFT: Picture books.
Classification: LCC PZ7.1.N683 Bad 2022 (print) | LCC PZ7.1.N683
(ebook) | DDC [Fic]—dc23
LC record available at https://lccn.loc.gov/2021056946
LC ebook record available at https://lccn.loc.gov/2021056947

Design Elements: Shutterstock/g_tech, Shutterstock/Olgastocker

Designed by Kay Fraser

TABLE OF CONTENTS

Meet Lola!

¡Hola, I'm Lola! I live in Texas with my family—Mama, Dad, and my baby sister, Mariana. The rest of my family, including my grandparents, live in Guatemala. That's where my parents are from. I know lots of interesting facts about the country.

Facts About Guatemala

- Guatemala is in Central America. It is about the size of the state of Tennessee.
- Guatemala has 37 volcanoes, but only three are active—that means they're erupting. The other 34 are asleep.
- The official language in Guatemala is Spanish.

Facts About Me

- I'm learning Spanish.
- I love history. I want to be an archaeologist when I grow up.
- I adore my family.
- I don't like change.
- I hate Mondays and onions, not to mention waking up early. Yuck!

My Family

Mama likes to speak Spanish at home. She is always trying to teach me about my roots and culture. Here are some other facts about Mama:

- She loves chocolate.
- She misses her family in Guatemala and wishes we saw them more often.
- She hates clutter!

Dad travels a lot for work. Since he is gone so much, our family time is extra special. Here are some other facts about Dad:

- He loves cars.
- He hates being late.
- He always makes us laugh!

Abuelita, my grandma, is one of my favorite people. She visits us once or twice a year. It is magical when we are together. She has the best stories. Here are some other facts about Abuelita:

- She cooks the best food and gives the best advice.
- She knows how to do just about anything.
- She is my favorite!

Abuelo, my grandpa, spends most of his time in Guatemala. (Don't tell anyone, but I think he is afraid of planes!) Here are some other facts about Abuelo:

- He loves Abuelita's cooking!
- He is always happy.
- He loves singing, telling jokes, and being playful.

Chapter 1

No Superstitions

The delicious smell of bacon and waffles woke me up in the morning. I knew what that meant—Sunday!

I loved Sundays. They were our special family time. Dad always made a yummy breakfast.

I hopped out of bed. The silver mirror Abuelita had given me on one of her visits sat on my dresser. It had been Abuelita's when she was my age.

I picked up the mirror and looked at my reflection. I missed my grandmother. We only saw each other twice a year, but we spoke on the phone every day. Holding the mirror reminded me of her.

"Lola, breakfast is ready!" Mama hollered from the kitchen.

"Coming!" I called back.

I placed the mirror on the corner of my dresser and darted out of my room. I was starving! But I bumped the dresser on my way past, and my mirror tumbled off.

Please let it be okay, I thought.

But as I picked up the mirror, my heart sank. The glass was cracked.

"NOOOOOO!" I exclaimed.

I wanted to cry. I couldn't believe I had broken something so special.

I shuffled downstairs with the mirror in my hand. Mama was video chatting with Abuelita. Dad was standing at the stove.

"Good morning, Lola!" Dad said. He set my plate on the kitchen table.

"Are you okay? I heard you yell," Mama said. She turned the computer toward me without waiting for an answer. "Abuelita wants to talk to you!"

"¡Hola, Lola! How are you today?" Abuelita asked.

I looked down at my feet. I didn't want to tell Abuelita about the broken mirror. I was worried she would be upset with me. But I knew I had to be honest.

"I broke the mirror you gave me, Abuelita," I confessed.

"Uh-oh." Abuelita chuckled. "Now, you'll have seven years of bad luck!"

"What?" I exclaimed. "I'm sorry! It was an accident!"

"Don't worry, Lola. That's just a superstition," Abuelita replied.

"Let me see," Mama said.

I handed her the mirror.

"It doesn't look that bad. We might be able to fix it," Mama told me.

"I know someone who can replace the glass," Dad offered.

But I was worried. *What if Abuelita is right?* I thought. *Am I going to have seven years of bad luck?*

I shook my head. I was being silly. Abuelita and my parents were always telling me leyendas—legends—from Guatemala.

Those are just stories, I reminded myself. Besides, I wasn't superstitious.

Mama hung up with Abuelita, and we sat down for breakfast. Normally I loved Dad's cooking, but it was hard to enjoy eating when I was worried.

After breakfast, we went to church. Mama and Dad had grown up going every Sunday in Guatemala. They wanted my sister and me to do the same.

When we got home that afternoon, we prepared a Sunday feast. Dad grilled steaks, and Mama made all the side dishes.

We had a dance party while we cooked. Mama loved dancing. She was always

teaching me how to dance salsa, merengue, and all the other Latin dances.

Dad twirled me around the living room. I was not paying attention and twirled right into the counter. I accidentally tipped over the saltshaker.

"Sorry!" I said.

"Don't worry. Grab a pinch of salt!" Mama told me.

I was confused, but I grabbed a tiny bit.

"A little sprinkle over your shoulder for good luck!" Mama said. She sprinkled some salt over her left shoulder. "You do it too, Lola."

I did as I was told. Then I looked around the room. I spotted Dad's jar of lucky pennies. My baby sister, Mariana, had a lucky toy monkey. Even I had a lucky rock.

Each member of my family had a lucky charm. Maybe we were superstitious after all. And if we were, then superstitions were real.

Abuelita's words from that morning flew
into my mind. A tiny seed of fear planted itself
in my heart. Had breaking the mirror given
me seven years of bad luck?

Chapter 2

Unlucky Number Seven

The next morning, I woke up and got ready for school. I brushed my hair and put on my favorite red bows. Then I spotted the broken mirror on my dresser.

I felt a knot in my tummy. Yesterday's tiny seed of fear was not so little anymore. Now it was sprouting. I tried to ignore it.

I am not superstitious, I reminded myself.

I went downstairs for breakfast. Mama had made champurradas—thin, crunchy cookies covered with white sesame seeds. They were delicious and tasted just like the ones I'd eaten when I visited Guatemala.

Cookies for breakfast—best day ever! I thought as I crunched on my treat.

After I ate, I walked to the bus stop with Mama and Mariana. But on the way, a black cat crossed the street in front of us.

"Look at the kitty, girls!" Mama said.

In her stroller, Mariana pointed and giggled. But I froze. A black cat was no laughing matter. It was bad luck!

I stared at the cat. First the broken mirror, and now this.

What if Abuelita is right? I worried. *Am I doomed to have seven years of bad luck?*

I tried to stay calm. *As long as I don't run into any more bad luck, I'll be okay,* I told myself.

We got to the bus stop and waited for a while. Mama checked her watch. Then she frowned and pulled out her phone.

"Oh, no!" she exclaimed.

"What is it?" I asked.

"My watch must have died. We're late and missed the bus!" Mama said.

Uh-oh, I thought. *More bad luck!*

"Let's run home," Mama said. "I'll have to drive you."

We rushed back home. I had never seen Mama run so fast with the stroller.

I hopped in the car as Mama buckled Mariana into her car seat. Off we drove.

There was a lot of traffic, and ALL the traffic lights were red.

Mama sighed. "It's like the world knows we are in a hurry!" she exclaimed. "We sure are having bad luck today, Lola!"

"Don't say that, Mama!" I whispered. "We don't want things to get worse."

"I'm just kidding," Mama said with a smile.

It's happening, I thought.

Mama might blame her watch, but I knew the truth. My bad luck was the reason we'd missed the bus. I just hoped the day didn't get worse.

Chapter 3

The Marbles

I made it to school just in time. I hurried to my classroom, placed my backpack in my cubby, and went to my seat. My friend Sophia waved to me from her desk as I sat down.

"Good morning, everyone!" my teacher, Ms. Bird, said. "I hope you all had a fun weekend. Who here likes food?"

All around the classroom, hands shot into the air.

Ms. Bird smiled. "Good. As we've learned, our country is made up of many different cultures. To celebrate that, we will have a culture day potluck this Friday, the thirteenth!"

Friday the thirteenth? I thought. Chills went down my spine. More bad luck!

"What's a potluck?" someone asked.

"It's a meal where everyone brings something to share," Ms. Bird explained. "I'd like you each to find out where your ancestors came from. Then bring a dish that represents that country or place. We'll enjoy all the different foods together over lunch."

I knew where my ancestors were from— Guatemala! Most of my family still lived there. There were lots of yummy dishes I could bring: tamales, tostadas, chuchitos, paches, enchiladas. . . . I didn't know how I'd choose just one!

I was writing a list of ideas when the lead in my pencil broke. I stood up to sharpen it.

I was so busy thinking of ideas that I wasn't paying attention. I bumped into Sophia's desk. A jar of marbles sitting on the edge of her desk wobbled and fell.

I gasped. The marbles *clicked-clacked-whooshed* all over the floor. Everyone turned and stared.

"My marbles!" Sophia exclaimed. She looked like she might cry. "I was supposed to talk about them for show-and-tell!"

I covered my face. "I'm sorry!" I replied.

I was so embarrassed. When I wasn't paying attention, my bad luck had struck again!

* * *

When I got home from school, Mama was video chatting with Abuelita.

"Hi, Mama," I said. "¡Hola, Abuelita!" I waved to the computer.

"How was school today?" Abuelita asked.

I hesitated. I wanted to tell her about my bad luck, but I wasn't ready to believe I was doomed for the next seven years. I would be a teenager by then!

I didn't mention that Friday was the thirteenth. Instead, I said, "Friday is culture day at school. We are having a potluck. I need to bring something Guatemalan."

"How about canillitas de leche?" Abuelita suggested.

"Great idea, Abuelita. Those are my favorite!" I cheered.

"Grab a paper and a pencil, I'll give you the recipe," Abuelita said.

I couldn't wait to learn how to make canillitas de leche! I usually only got to have

the yummy milk candies when Abuelita came
to visit. Making them at home would be like
she was here!

I ran to the other room to get some paper.
When I came back, Abuelita started listing the
ingredients.

"You'll need a can of condensed milk, a cup
of powdered milk, a cup of cornstarch, and a
big bowl . . ." Abuelita said.

I wrote as fast as I could.

"Thank you, Abuelita," I said when she was
finished. "Everyone is going to love them!"

"Good luck!" Abuelita replied, blowing kisses.

I didn't want to think about luck, but that put it back in my head. Luck was everywhere!

Maybe if I had my lucky rock with me, things would get better. I ran upstairs and opened my nightstand. There it was—Suerte, my lucky rock. I had found it on a hiking trip a long time ago.

I placed Suerte in my pocket. It was heavy, but I felt better. I just hoped my lucky rock was enough to protect me against my bad luck.

Chapter 4

The Rock of Doom

The next day at school, I had my lucky rock with me. I was not superstitious, but a little extra luck couldn't hurt. More was always better. More chocolate in my ice cream? Delicious! More cheese on my pizza? Yum! A little extra luck? Yes, please!

At recess, I hurried to the secret garden area where my friends and I usually played. I spotted Joy. She was one of the first people I'd met at this school.

"Joy!" I called, waving to my friend. "I have something to show you!"

Joy hurried over. She looked excited. "What is it?"

"My lucky rock, Suerte!" I said.

Suerte had made itself at home inside my pocket. When I took out my rock, it was covered with lint and pencil shavings. I tried to brush it off, but the rock was so smooth it slipped right out of my hand.

I crouched down to grab Suerte. Joy bent down at the same time. I didn't realize she was standing right above me. As I lifted my head, it bumped Joy right in the face—hard.

"Ouch!" Joy hollered. "My nose!"

"Are you okay?" I asked.

Joy shook her head. She had tears in her eyes. Her nose was starting to swell.

"I'm sorry!" I said.

I helped Joy to the nurse. I had hurt one of my best friends. It had been an accident, but that didn't make me feel better.

"I don't think your nose is broken," the nurse said to Joy. "But I'll call your parents just to be safe. They might want to pick you up and take you for an X-ray."

I didn't know what to say. If it weren't for me, Joy would be fine right now. My bad luck was spreading *everywhere*.

The nurse dismissed me back to class. I walked slowly down the hallway.

When I reached my classroom, I paused. I took the lucky rock out of my pocket. Suerte meant luck, but my bad luck had turned even my lucky rock *un*lucky! After today my rock needed a new name. It was more like the rock of doom!

Chapter 5

The Spill

I rode the bus home alone that afternoon. Joy usually rode it too, but she had gone home early. I spent the whole ride hoping my luck would change somehow. Things were getting worse!

When I got home, I took off my shoes and backpack. My soccer ball was sitting by the front door. I grabbed it and dribbled it between my feet.

"I'm home!" I called.

"In here, mija!" Mama replied.

I dribbled into the living room. Mama was reading a book and having a glass of limeade. Mariana was strapped into her bouncy chair.

My little sister pointed at my feet. "Ball!" she said proudly.

"Good, Mariana!" I said. I rolled the ball gently to her.

Mama gave me a look. "Are you supposed to be playing ball inside?" she said.

"My bad," I said. "I'll put it away."

I kicked the ball toward the doorway, but my aim was off. The ball bounced off the doorframe and flew toward the coffee table. It knocked into the pitcher of limeade sitting there. The sweet drink spilled *everywhere*.

"Lola!" Mama cried. "What did I just say?"

"I'm sorry!" I exclaimed. "It was an accident."

"Quick! Go get a mop to clean this up," Mama said. She carefully moved Mariana away from the spill.

"I'm cursed!" I wailed. "It's all because I broke Abuelita's mirror!"

"This has nothing to do with luck, mija," Mama replied. "Now hurry. We have to clean this up."

I went to the closet where we kept all the cleaning supplies. I reached in and grabbed a handle, thinking it was a mop. But when I pulled it out, it was an umbrella. It popped open—inside the house.

I shrieked. Opening an umbrella inside the house was bad luck!

"Mama! Mamiiiiii!" I hollered.

I ran back to the living room. I was so upset that I didn't even notice the ladder Dad had

out to replace the battery in the smoke alarm. I ducked right under it.

It took me a moment to realize what I'd just done. *Oh no!* I thought. *Walking under a ladder is bad luck too!*

"What happened?" Mama asked. "Why were you yelling?"

"I accidentally opened an umbrella inside the house!" I confessed. "And now I walked under the ladder!"

"Oh, Lola. Don't believe those superstitions!" Mama comforted me.

But I had the list of bad things running through my head:

1. *I'd broken a mirror.*
2. *A black cat had crossed my path.*
3. *I'd missed the bus.*
4. *I'd spilled Sophia's marbles.*
5. *I'd almost broken Joy's nose.*
6. *I'd kicked my soccer ball straight into the pitcher of limeade.*
7. *I'd opened an umbrella in the house.*
8. *I'd walked under the ladder.*

I was well on my way to having bad luck for SEVEN YEARS, and it was only Tuesday.

Chapter 6

Lucky Charm

Wednesday morning at school, Ms. Bird reminded us about Friday's potluck.

"Let's go around the room and talk about what everyone is planning to bring," she suggested. "Make sure it's something that represents where your family comes from."

"My family is from Ireland. I'm bringing cheese!" Owen said.

"My family is from Italy. I'm bringing pasta!" said Francesca.

"I'm bringing canillitas de leche," I announced. "They're a special treat from Guatemala. My abuelita gave me the recipe!"

"I'm looking forward to tasting them," Ms. Bird said. "What about you, Sophia?"

"I don't know yet," Sophia answered nervously.

"That's okay," Ms. Bird said. "We still have a couple of days. Everyone, remember to give your parents the note in your folder tonight. All the details are in there."

When it was time for recess, Sophia asked, "Do you want to go to the secret garden?"

I paused. I wanted to play with my friends, but I was worried. Joy probably already blamed me for hurting her nose, and I was sure Sophia was mad about her marbles.

"No thanks," I said. I hurried away.

"Why not?" Sophia called after me.

I pretended not to hear.

Joy was sitting at one of the outdoor benches. She waved to get my attention.

"Lola, over here!" she called.

I didn't want to cause Joy any more problems. I just smiled and went in another direction. Joy frowned.

I found a quiet area to play on my own. It wasn't as much fun without my two best friends. I kicked the grass, and when I looked down, I saw a four-leaf clover.

Yes! I thought. *Four-leaf clovers are lucky!*

My luck was about to change. I could feel it.

But then I felt something else—the *whoosh* of a soccer ball flying at me.

"Lola, watch out!" someone shouted.

But it was too late. The ball smacked into me. It knocked the four-leaf clover out of my hand. Then the ball bounced right on top of it.

Soccer balls are bad luck too! I thought.

I stared down at the crushed clover. *NOOO!* What could be worse luck than destroying a lucky charm?

I walked back to my class with my head down. From the corner of my eye, I saw Joy and Sophia. I kept walking. My bad luck was contagious. It was rubbing off on everything. And I didn't want it to rub off on my friends.

During science that afternoon, Ms. Bird told us to partner up.

"Let's work together," Sophia said. She scooted her desk closer.

I shook my head. "I can't," I replied.

I went to the other side of the classroom. Sophia looked upset.

Finally, the bell rang. I hurried to catch the bus. But Joy caught up to me as we were getting on.

"Are you okay?" she asked. "You've been acting weird all day."

"I have to go," I said.

I sat as far away from Joy as I could. The whole way home, I stared out the window, feeling lonely.

The way things were going, there was no way I could participate in Friday's potluck—not on Friday the thirteenth. With me there, it would be a pot of *bad* luck.

Look on the Bright Side

I was extra cautious when I got home from school that day. I ran straight up to my room. I closed my curtains and hid under my covers. Maybe if I stayed in my room alone, I would be safe. Then my bad luck couldn't spread anywhere else.

A while later, Mama called up to me from the kitchen. "Lola, dinner is ready!"

"I'm not hungry!" I hollered back.

"Come downstairs now, please. Before dinner gets cold!" Mama said.

I sighed and threw off my covers. I *was* a little hungry.

I peeked out of my bedroom door like I was crossing a street. I looked left, then right. No bad luck in either direction.

Then I crept downstairs. I grabbed onto the railing for dear life. It was just a matter of time before something else unlucky happened.

Dad, Mama, and Mariana were already seated at the dining table. I tiptoed into the room like I was walking on eggshells.

"What are you playing, Lola?" Mama asked.

"Nothing, I'm just being extra careful today," I said.

"Do you want me to get you a giant hamster ball to roll around inside?" Mama chuckled.

"Not a bad idea," I muttered.

"Seriously, what is going on?" Mama asked.

"I'm cursed!" I exclaimed. "I'm going to have seven years of bad luck. And it's already started."

"Is this because of the broken mirror?"
Mama asked.

I nodded.

"You know Abuelita was joking about
that!" Mama exclaimed.

"But it's happening, Mama! Ever since
I broke the mirror, I've seen bad luck
everywhere. First, it was that black cat.
Then, I missed the bus. And then—"

Mama stopped me. "You know what your abuelita always told me? A mal tiempo, buena cara—you have to look on the bright side. You had a bad day. Tomorrow will be better."

"What about all the bad luck I've had?" I insisted.

"Accidents and 'bad luck' happen to everyone," Mama replied. "You have to try to learn from the experience."

"But everything I touch breaks. Even when I found a four-leaf clover, it got smashed at recess!" I exclaimed. "And I'm pretty sure Joy and Sophia don't want to be friends with me anymore."

"Why would you think that?" Mama asked.

"Because of my bad luck!" I exclaimed. "It made me knock over Sophia's marbles at school. And then thanks to my *lucky* rock, Joy hurt her nose."

"Did you talk to them and apologize?" Dad asked.

I looked down at my feet. "No," I admitted. "I avoided them."

"Ignoring your problems is never a solution," Mama said. "If you hurt your friends or their feelings, you need to take responsibility and apologize."

"I was trying to keep them safe," I insisted. "My bad luck is spilling all over the place. I didn't want it to rub off on them."

"It doesn't sound like bad luck is to blame, Lola," Dad said. "It sounds like the way you *treated* your friends is what has them upset with you."

I frowned. My dad had a point, but still . . .

"I don't think I should go to the potluck at school on Friday," I said. "It's too risky. It's Friday the thirteenth!"

"Friday the thirteenth is just a regular day," Mama said. "You can't look for signs of bad luck everywhere. Why don't you look for blessings instead?"

"Your mama is right," Dad chimed in. "Seven years of bad luck, black cats, and Friday the thirteenth are just superstitions, like leyendas."

I sighed. "I don't know . . ."

"Let me tell you a story," Dad said. "Once, when I was growing up in Guatemala, my friends and I went to Lake Atitlán. Late at night, we were telling leyendas. I saw a shadow. I was sure it was a ghost. I told the ghost I was not scared and to go away. But the truth is, I was terrified."

I couldn't imagine Dad being scared. "What did you do?" I asked.

"The shadow started to move toward me. I wanted to run away, but fear had me frozen. The shadow got closer and closer," Dad said slowly.

"Then what happened?" I asked.

"I heard laughter," Dad replied. "And I realized the truth. The 'ghost' was just a

person admiring the lake at night. I learned an important lesson. Leyendas are a fun tradition—until you take them too seriously."

"The same thing goes for superstitions," Mama said. "You can't let them get into your head and scare you."

"I'll try," I promised.

My parents were right. I couldn't let bad luck take over. It was time to focus on the positive.

Chapter 8

The Secret Ingredient

The next morning, the smell of chocolate caliente drifted upstairs. That was one of Abuelita's favorite recipes. Could she be here? I hurried downstairs to investigate.

"¡Buenos días, Lola!" Mama said.

"Morning, Mama," I replied. "For a second, I thought Abuelita was here. It smells like her chocolate caliente!"

"I know her recipe by heart," Mama told me. "The secret ingredient is amor—love! I wanted you to have a good start to your day."

We sipped a bit of chocolate. The sweet drink felt like a warm hug from Abuelita.

I smiled at Mama. "Thank you. This is delicious!"

"Today is going to be a better day, Lola," Mama said.

I nodded. "I hope so. I'm going to start by apologizing to Joy and Sophia."

"I'm proud of you, mija," Mama said. She gave me a hug. "That's very mature."

"Maybe I could have them over today," I suggested. "We have to make the canillitas de leche for the potluck. It would be fun to make them with my friends."

"That's a great idea!" Mama said. "You talk to Joy and Sophia at school. I'll call their parents and make sure it's okay."

I smiled. My luck was turning around. I would make sure of it.

* * *

Joy didn't sit with me on the bus to school. I smiled at her, but she ignored me. When I got to class, Sophia didn't say hi like she usually does.

I felt sad. I missed my friends. I needed to fix this!

At recess, I went to the secret garden. Sophia and Joy were already there. They both frowned when I walked up.

"What are you doing here?" Joy asked. "I thought you didn't want us to be your friends anymore."

I was nervous, but I knew what I had to do. "I came to say sorry," I said.

"Why did you ignore us yesterday?" Sophia asked.

"I was convinced I was bringing you both bad luck," I answered. "I broke a mirror my abuelita gave me, and she told me it meant seven years of bad luck. She was joking, but I started seeing bad luck *everywhere.*"

"Like what?" Joy asked.

"Like me showing you my lucky rock and almost breaking your nose," I said. I turned

to Sophia. "And when I knocked over your jar of marbles!"

"Those were accidents," said Joy.

"Yeah," Sophia agreed. "I just didn't like being ignored all day!"

"I'm sorry," I said. "I thought if I stayed away from you, my bad luck wouldn't spread. But I learned that I can't take superstitions too seriously. Accidents happen to everyone. What matters is that I take responsibility and learn from my mistakes. I'll be more careful."

"As long as we are together, we'll be okay!" Joy said.

"Group hug!" cheered Sophia.

I was happy to be back to normal with my BFFs.

"Do you want to come to my house this afternoon?" I asked. "Mama and I are making Guatemalan candy for tomorrow's potluck."

"Definitely!" said Joy. "I wish my class was having a potluck."

"That sounds fun," Sophia agreed.

"Yay!" I cheered. "My mama is going to call your parents to ask if it's okay."

"Let's cross our fingers that they say yes!" Joy said.

When we came in after recess, Ms. Bird called Sophia and me to the front of the room.

"Sophia, your mom called the office," she told us. "You're going to ride the bus home with Lola today."

Sophia and I exchanged grins. My luck was changing!

I counted the minutes, waiting for the day to end. When the bell finally rang, Sophia and I ran to the bus.

Joy was already there. She greeted us with a giant smile. "Guess what? I'm going to Lola's house too!" she exclaimed.

This is the best bus ride ever, I decided. I had my two best friends with me. Having them was all the luck I needed.

Chapter 9

Cooking Class

When Sophia, Joy, and I got to my house, my little sister was bouncing up and down in her chair. She greeted us with a huge smile.

"Hi, Mariana!" I kissed her.

"Welcome, girls!" Mama said. "Ready to make some candy?"

"Yes!" we all cheered.

"Then let's get started," Mama said. "First things first. We need to wash our hands."

My friends and I all used the sink to clean up. Mama put on her apron. Then it was time to get to work!

Mama had set out all the ingredients to make canillitas de leche. With her help, we mixed condensed milk, powdered milk,

powdered sugar, and cornstarch in a bowl. We made a very sticky dough. At first, it was too runny. Then it looked like goo. After mixing and mixing, we finally got it right.

"Now what?" Joy asked.

"Now we roll it out," said Mama.

She spread parchment paper on the kitchen counter and sprinkled it with cornstarch. Then, she set the dough on top.

Mama passed the cornstarch to us. "Rub some on your hands so you can work with the dough," she explained. "You don't want it to stick."

Joy giggled as she rubbed her hands together. "This is fun!"

Mama rubbed some cornstarch on the rolling pin too. Then she rolled the dough until it was smooth and flat.

"Grab the butter knife and sprinkle some cornstarch on it," Mama said. "It's time to cut the dough into strips."

"Can I go first?" Sophia asked.

"Sure!" I said.

"Like this—about as big as a finger," Mama said, showing us.

Joy, Sophia, and I all took turns cutting the dough into strips.

"Those look perfect!" Mama told us.

"Can we try some?" Joy asked.

"Not yet. Canillitas de leche are supposed to be hard. They need to air-dry," Mama said.

"But Abuelita always says that the best part about cooking is sampling what you make," I said with a giggle.

Mama smiled. "I suppose one little bite wouldn't hurt."

We each took a tiny bite of the soft dough.

"Mmm! Sweet and gooey!" said Joy.

"They are delicious!" Sophia declared.

We set the canillitas de leche on the counter to dry. I was excited to see what my classmates thought about the homemade candy. The potluck was going to be great!

Chapter 10

The Potluck

Lucky Friday the thirteenth, I thought as I got ready for school the next day.

I had stayed up late the night before helping Mama make sure the canillitas de leche were perfect. I was not leaving anything to chance. There would be no accidents or bad luck today.

I hopped on the bus feeling hopeful. Nothing bad happened on my way to school! The plastic container holding my Guatemalan treats was so well-packed that I wasn't even worried about something spilling.

When I got to my classroom, there were so many different foods and scents. It smelled delicious!

"Students, please place your dishes at the table over in that corner," Ms. Bird instructed.

"I can't wait for everyone to try the canillitas de leche!" I whispered to Sophia. "What did you bring?"

"I found out that my great grandfather was French. I brought croissants!" Sophia replied.

"Have a seat, please!" Ms. Bird said to the class. "It smells delicious in here. I can't wait to hear about what you all brought."

"Let's eat!" someone said.

Ms. Bird smiled. "We'll enjoy the food together over lunch," she reminded us. "Be patient. The morning will fly by!"

We had math and gym in the morning. It was hard to focus with all the delicious smells. Finally, it was lunchtime.

Everyone had a story about the foods they brought and the different places their ancestors had come from. I was excited to try a little bit of everything!

Then it was my turn.

"These are homemade milk candies. They are called canillitas de leche. That means little milk legs!" I said.

Everyone laughed.

"They are my favorite candy from Guatemala. That's where my family is from. Sophia and Joy helped me make them yesterday after school. We used my abuelita's recipe!" I continued.

Everyone grabbed one and then came back for more. The canillitas de leche were a success! *Luckily*, I had enough for everyone to have seconds.

* * *

At home, I told my parents all about the potluck. "Everyone loved the canillitas de leche!" I said.

Mama smiled. "I'm so happy to hear that!"

"Time to celebrate! Let's go out to eat," Dad proposed.

We went to my favorite Chinese restaurant for dinner. At the end of the meal, the server brought four fortune cookies.

I tore open the plastic wrapper and cracked open my cookie. "You'll have seven years of good luck!" I read aloud.

I smiled. I didn't believe in bad luck, but more good luck never hurt!

GLOSSARY

accident (AK-suh-duhnt)—a sudden and unexpected event that leads to loss or injury

ancestor (AN-sess-tur)—a family member who lived a long time ago

avoid (uh-VOYD)—to stay away from something

contagious (kun-TAY-juss)—easy to catch or spread

croissant (krwuh-SAHNT)—a crescent-shaped French bread roll made from buttered layers of yeast dough

culture (KUHL-chuhr)—a people's way of life, ideas, customs, and traditions

legend (LEJ-uhnd)—a story handed down from earlier times; legends are often based on fact, but they are not entirely true

mature (muh-CHOOR)—to act in a sensible, grown-up kind of way

parchment (PARCH-muhnt)—a strong, heat-resistant paper used to keep food from sticking to a pan

potluck (POT-luhk)—a meal to which people bring food to share

superstition (soo-pur-STIH-shuhn)—a belief that an action can affect the outcome of a future event

SPANISH GLOSSARY

abuelita (ah-bweh-LEE-tah)—grandmother

amor (ah-MOHR)—love

buenos días (BWEH-nohs DEE-ahs)—good morning

canillatas de leche (kah-nee-YEE-tahs deh LEH-cheh)—sweets made with powdered sugar and milk

champurradas (chahm-poo-RRAH-dahs)—thin, crunchy cookies covered with white sesame seeds

chocolate caliente (choh-koh-LAH-teh kah-LYEHN-teh)—hot chocolate

hola (OH-lah)—hello

leyenda (leh-YEHN-dah)—legend

mija (MEE-ha)—Spanish for "my daughter" but can also be used as a term of affection meaning "my child," "dear," or "honey"

suerte (SWEHR-teh)—luck

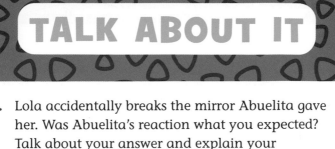

TALK ABOUT IT

1. Lola accidentally breaks the mirror Abuelita gave her. Was Abuelita's reaction what you expected? Talk about your answer and explain your reasoning.

2. Even though she says she's not superstitious, Lola is convinced she will have seven years of bad luck. She starts seeing bad luck everywhere! Do you believe in luck? Why or why not?

3. Why do you think Lola was so sure her bad luck was going to rub off on her friends? Talk about it, then discuss some other ways she could have handled things.

WRITE IT DOWN

1. Lola realizes that everyone in her house has a lucky charm. Do you have any good luck charms at home? First, make a list of them, then pick one and describe why it's lucky. If you don't have any, pick one from the story to write about.

2. What dish would you bring to a culture day potluck? Ask a parent, grandparent, or guardian about your ancestors. Then write a paragraph about where your family comes from and the food you chose to represent that place.

3. Joy and Sophia are both hurt when Lola starts ignoring them. Imagine you are in Joy or Sophia's position. Pick one of the characters and write a letter to Lola from that person's point of view, explaining how you feel.

LOLA'S CANILLITAS DE LECHE

Canillitas de leche are one of Lola's favorite Guatemalan treats. With an adult's help, try making these sweet treats at home.

WHAT YOU NEED

- 1 can condensed milk (14 ounces)
- ½ cup powdered sugar
- 1 cup powdered milk
- 1 cup cornstarch
- a large mixing bowl
- a big spoon
- parchment paper
- a butter knife
- a rolling pin

WHAT TO DO

1. Combine condensed milk, powdered sugar, powdered milk, and half of the cornstarch in a mixing bowl. Mix all ingredients until smooth. It should look like cookie dough.

2. Spread out a sheet of parchment paper. Sprinkle remaining cornstarch on top. (Get some on your hands, the rolling pin, and the knife too. This will keep the dough from sticking.)

3. Place the dough on top of the parchment paper. With the rolling pin, roll the dough on top of the parchment paper.

4. Using the knife, cut the dough into pieces about 2 inches long and 1/3-inch wide, or about as thick as your finger.

5. Let the strips of dough air-dry. Once they are hard, your canillitas de leche are ready to eat!

Tip: Use any leftover dough to form circles about the size of a silver dollar. Sprinkle some cinnamon on top, and you can make encaneladas, another Guatemalan treat!

ABOUT THE AUTHOR

Keka Novales grew up in Guatemala City, Guatemala, which is located in Central America. Growing up, she wanted to be a doctor, a vet, a ballerina, an engineer, and a writer. Keka moved several times and changed schools, so she has plenty of experience being the "new kid." Her grandparents had a vital role in her life. Abuelo was always making jokes, and Abuelita was helping everyone around her. Keka currently lives with her family in Denton, Texas.

ABOUT THE ILLUSTRATOR

Gloria Félix was born and raised in Uruapan, a beautiful, small city in Michoacán, Mexico. Her home is one of her biggest inspirations when it comes to art. Her favorite things to do growing up were drawing, watching cartoons, and eating, which still are some of her favorite things to do. Gloria currently lives and paints in Los Angeles, California.